At the Beginning of a Pig

A foldout flap book

Nicola Moon ● Andy Ellis

Kingfisher

NEW YORK

At the beginning of a pig
there's a snuffling snout,

At the beginning of a crocodile
there's a wicked grin,

At the beginning of a rabbit
there's a twitching nose,

At the beginning of a dog
there's a wet and shiny sniffer,

At the beginning of a cat
    there's a green eye and a whisker,

At the beginning of a snake
there's a hissing tongue that flickers,

At the beginning of a monkey
there's a playful pair of eyes,

At the beginning of an elephant
there's a long gray trunk,

At the beginning of a child
there's a face that's full of fun,